THE CREEPY CLASSICS CHILDREN'S COLLECTION

Dados Internacionais de Catalogação na Publicação (CIP) de acordo com ISBD

W671t Wilde, Oscar.
The Picture Of Dorian Gray / Oscar Wilde. - Jandira, SP : W. Books, 2025.
120 p. ; 12,80cm x 19,80cm. - (Classics).

ISBN: 978-65-5294-193-0

1. Literatura inglesa. 2. Clássicos. 3. Fantasia. 4. Imaginação. 5. Terror.
6. Suspense. I. Título. II. Série

2025-2531 CDD 823
CDU 811.131-1

Elaborada por Lucio Feitosa - CRB-8/8803
Índice para catálogo sistemático:
1. Literatura inglesa 823.
2. Literatura inglesa 821.111-31

Text based on the original story by Oscar Wilde,
adapted by Gemma Barder
Illustrations by Nick Moffatt

1st edition in 2025
www.cirandacultural.com.br

THE PICTURE OF DORIAN GRAY

OSCAR WILDE

W. Books

DORIAN GRAY
A handsome young man

BASIL HALLWARD
A painter

Lord Henry

A rich man

Sibyl Vane

An actress

James Vane

Sibyl's brother

Chapter One

'I think this is the best painting you've ever done,' said Lord Henry, standing back to admire the canvas his friend, Basil Hallward, was working on.

Basil continued setting out his paints and getting his studio ready for the afternoon. The painting was not quite finished,

but he had to admit, he agreed with Lord Henry.

'There's only one bad thing I can think to say about it,' Lord Henry added, stroking his dark, pointed beard. 'It's *too* perfect. The young man in this painting is far too handsome to be real.'

Basil chuckled. 'But the young man *is* real,' he said. 'His name is Dorian Gray. He recently inherited his grandfather's fortune and a house in London. He is becoming quite popular.'

'Dorian Gray!' cried Lord Henry. 'I've heard my Aunt Agatha talk about him!' Lord Henry came from a large, wealthy family. If there was anyone worth knowing in London, he was bound to find out about them. It annoyed him slightly that Basil had met the famous Dorian Gray before him. 'How did you meet?' he asked, reluctantly.

'At a party,' said Basil. 'When I first saw him, I was struck by how handsome he was. I asked if he'd ever had his portrait painted. He said no, so I offered to do it for him.'

Lord Henry turned back to the

portrait
A painting or drawing of a person, usually only the head and shoulders.

painting. The face was bright, with striking blue eyes. Golden hair crowned the head in waves, and even though the figure was seated, you could tell that it was tall. 'You should put this in a gallery so more people can see it.'

Basil blushed and shook his head. 'I can't,' he said. 'I promised to give the painting to Dorian. If he likes it, of course.'

At that moment, the doorbell chimed.

'Ah, that will be Dorian now. He is coming for his last sitting,' said Basil, fussing about his studio to make everything perfect for his guest. 'Perhaps you should go, Henry?'

Lord Henry placed his hands on his hips in mock fury. 'Are you trying to get rid of me, old friend?

I'm not going anywhere. I want to meet this famous young man to see if he really is as handsome as his portrait.'

Basil smiled, but secretly he sighed. He had been friends with Lord Henry for many years, and he knew what he was like. Lord Henry had to know everything that went on and everyone in town. But Basil liked having Dorian all to himself.

CHAPTER TWO

When Dorian Gray entered the studio, Lord Henry was amazed. The young man was just as handsome – if not more handsome – than Basil's portrait made him out to be.

'May I introduce my friend Lord Henry,' said Basil, a little reluctantly.

'Pleased to meet you,' said Dorian, holding out his hand. He was friendly and confident, and

he wore expensive, fashionable clothes. Lord Henry, who knew all the best places to shop, was immediately impressed.

'It's good to finally put a face to the name,' he said. 'My Aunt Agatha had you at one of her parties and has told me all about you!'

Dorian smiled. Basil hoped that Lord Henry would leave. The portrait was nearly finished and this would be the last time Dorian came to visit him. He wanted to be alone with his new friend.

'Shall I leave you to it?' asked Lord Henry, but he made no move to pick up his hat and gloves.

'Oh, I'm sure Basil won't mind if you stay,' said Dorian. 'It would be nice to have an audience, don't you think?'

Basil forced a smile and nodded. 'Of course,' he said, picking up his brushes as Dorian perched on a stool in front of him. Lord Henry sat back down on the sofa.

As Basil worked, Lord Henry decided to find out as much as he could about the young man. He asked him what plays he liked, what books he had read, who he had met and where he liked to eat.

It was not long before Lord Henry concluded that Dorian Gray had excellent taste in everything.

'I envy you,' said Lord Henry. 'You're young and you still have the whole world to enjoy. Food, drink, fashion, people and parties – everything is yours for the taking!'

'No one can enjoy *everything* the world has to offer,' said Basil. 'They would get sick, or at least be thrown in jail.'

Dorian laughed.

'I don't agree,' Lord Henry continued. 'I believe that the only thing wrong with this world is that we're told to feel bad about what we want. It's a waste of time. If no one felt bad about anything, we would all be happier!'

Basil sighed. He did not like this side of his friend, but as Lord Henry got older, he seemed to care less and less about rules and manners. Basil decided to stop the conversation.

'The painting is finished,' he said, turning his attention back to Dorian. 'Would you like to see it?'

Chapter Three

Basil carefully turned the canvas to show Dorian the portrait. Lord Henry clasped his hands together in delight as Dorian stared in amazement.

'What do you think?' asked Basil, a little nervously. He could not read the expression on Dorian's face and he found the silence unsettling.

'It's … incredible – *wonderful*,' Dorian said at last. 'But it … it makes me a little sad …'

'Sad?' exclaimed Lord Henry. 'If I looked like you, I would never have a day's sadness in my life!'

Dorian smiled weakly. 'It's just that I'm twenty years old now, and I know that in all my life I will never look as good as I do in this painting. I wish … I wish that this painting could grow old instead of me. That I could stay just as you have painted me.'

Lord Henry clapped. 'Well said, young man! What a fabulous

idea! A portrait that ages instead of the person. Perhaps Basil can invent one?'

'I'm a painter, not an inventor,' said Basil, seriously. 'Dorian, as you grow older, you grow wiser. It's not always a bad thing to get wrinkles or the odd grey hair – it shows that you have lived a good life.' The look on Dorian's face worried Basil. He was staring at the painting with a mixture of fascination and terror.

'All this talk of ageing is upsetting me!' Lord Henry laughed. 'Why don't we all go to the theatre to take our minds off it? My carriage is just outside and the play at the Royal Theatre is meant to be very good.'

'Yes,' said Dorian, his face brightening. 'That sounds like just the right thing!'

'Not for me,' said Basil. He'd had enough of Lord Henry's company for the day. 'I must tidy up.'

Lord Henry thanked Basil for the interesting afternoon and made his way out of the studio.

'Mr Hallward, thank you so much for the portrait. It truly is wonderful. Are you sure I can have it?' asked Dorian, as they walked towards the front door of Basil's home.

'Of course,' said Basil. 'I will have it framed and sent over to your lovely new house.'

Dorian's face filled with joy. 'You're too kind, Mr Hallward! How can I repay you?'

'You can start by calling me Basil,' he replied. 'Also, my friend Lord Henry can be a little ... *over enthusiastic* about life. His views are odd and he talks

nonsense a lot of the time. Take care when you are with him. He can be a bad influence.'

Dorian nodded, before heading out the door and climbing into Lord Henry's carriage. Basil felt a wave of dread wash over him as he watched it pull away into the evening air.

CHAPTER FOUR

Despite Basil's warning, Dorian began spending a lot of time with Lord Henry. Unlike Basil, who tended to worry about small things and spent most of his evenings at home, Lord Henry was carefree and liked being around people. Dorian was often invited to the same dinners, plays and dances as Lord Henry, so they had plenty of opportunities to meet.

One night, at his Aunt Agatha's

house, Lord Henry sat close to Dorian and pointed out all the interesting people around the dinner table. '*He* is a friend of the king's,' said Lord Henry, secretly pointing at an older man. 'And *she* owns the largest department store in London ...'

Dorian took in each new, rich and interesting person. Everyone wanted to know about *him*, too, and Dorian was excited to be part of the fashionable London crowd.

'All the people here are like antiques,' said Lord Henry, loudly. So loudly that the other guests

stopped their own conversations to listen to him.

'I beg your pardon?' said a woman wearing a diamond necklace. 'Are you calling me an antique?' She sounded cross.

'I am,' said Lord Henry, boldly. 'You all are.'

Offended muttering rippled around the table. Lord Henry was being rude, but Dorian was thrilled by it. He remembered what Lord Henry had said the first time they met: *If no one felt bad about anything, we would all be happier.* It was true. Lord

Henry did not care what he said, and he was happy.

'You're antiques because you're beautiful and one of a kind!' he added. 'And I would buy any of you at auction!'

The dinner party guests began to laugh. Lord Henry had insulted them, but he'd followed it up with charm and flattery. Dorian was fascinated.

'I wonder which one of us would fetch the highest price,' said a gentleman with a curled moustache.

'Why the duchess, of course!'

replied Lord Henry, instantly.

The woman in question blushed and replied, 'Is that because the oldest antiques are the most expensive?'

'You're not old!' Lord Henry insisted, although the secret wink he gave Dorian suggested he was lying. 'You're still young enough to blush, aren't you?'

'Is blushing enough to make me young again?' the duchess asked, patting her papery pink cheeks.

Lord Henry shook his head. 'You also have to repeat the mistakes of the past; it is only when people try to do what's right that they become old and boring.'

'An interesting idea ...'

This "interesting idea" led to Lord Henry insisting that most people died of common sense, and other, wilder things that amused and shocked his listeners equally. No one listened closer than Dorian – and no one was more charmed.

He wanted to be like Lord Henry, who cared more about having fun than being proper, and who urged Dorian to live his life as he chose – while he was still young enough to enjoy it.

Chapter Five

Basil always felt uncomfortable in Lord Henry's sitting room. It was crammed with dark velvet furniture, and there were so many gold trinkets and crystal glasses that the surfaces seemed to sparkle. He sipped his drink and waited for their

friend, Dorian, to arrive. It had been two months since Basil had finished the portrait, and in that time Dorian and Lord Henry had become great friends and regulars at parties together.

When Dorian called Basil to tell him he had some exciting news, he asked if they could meet at Lord Henry's house.

'What is all this about?' asked Basil.

Lord Henry yawned and stretched out on one of his many red sofas in front of the roaring fire. 'I have no idea,' he said. 'I have not seen the boy for two weeks. It's like he disappeared into thin air.'

'I thought you two went everywhere together,' said Basil, grumpily.

'He reminds me of me when I was younger,' said Lord Henry. 'Although he's far better looking than I ever was – even at twenty!'

Basil was about to agree when one of Lord Henry's footmen announced Dorian's arrival.

'Friends, friends, I'm so glad you're here,' Dorian said. 'I have

footman
A servant whose job was to open doors and run errands around the house.

good news! I am going to be married!'

The two older men stared at Dorian. Basil wished he could share Dorian's happiness, but he was too stunned to speak. Lord Henry scoffed. 'Married?' he said, as though Dorian had just told him he was thinking of dying his hair blue. 'To whom?'

Dorian sat down and took off his hat. His cheeks were flushed and he looked happier and younger than ever. 'Her name is Sibyl and she's an actress,' Dorian began. 'I was in a not so nice part of town when I walked past a small theatre. It was so run down I simply had to go in to see if it was as awful inside as out. Oh! I have never seen such a performance! Sibyl played the character of Rosalind in *As You Like It*. I always thought Shakespeare was boring – but she made his work come alive!

'She was so good that I went back to watch her the next night, and the next, until I finally decided I had to speak to her. She is such a sweet and innocent girl, and when she *acts* she is magnificent! When we are married, I'm going to buy a theatre in the West End just for her!'

Basil and Lord Henry glanced at each other. Their young friend was clearly very much in love, but his engagement had happened worryingly fast.

'Well, congratulations …' said Basil. 'When can we meet the lady?'

'Tonight!' said Dorian, standing suddenly. 'She is about to play Juliet in *Romeo and Juliet* and I want you both to come to the theatre with me!'

Chapter Six

Sibyl Vane was eighteen years old. She came from a poor family and had always dreamt of a better life. As she strolled through the

park with her older brother, she sighed dreamily. 'Oh James, did you ever imagine my life would be so wonderful?' she said.

James remained silent. He was dressed in a sailor's uniform and carried a large bag of his belongings on his shoulder.

That afternoon, he was due to set sail with the Royal Navy.

'Just think, soon I will be Mrs Gray and living in one of the finest houses in London!' Sibyl continued. 'I won't have to return to that dingy little theatre ever again.'

'He should have asked for your family's permission before he asked you to marry him,' James said. 'We've never even met him. Does he think he can do what he likes, just because he has money and we don't?'

Sibyl laughed. 'You are so old fashioned, James! Dorian is a good man. I'm sure he will meet you all in good time. And when we're married, I shall invite you all to stay in my fancy house. Oh, I can't wait!'

James frowned. He wished that he did not have to set sail so soon. He wanted to meet this Dorian Gray in person. Sibyl was a sweet girl. She always saw the best in people, but James knew more about the world than she did. As her older brother, he felt that it was his job to protect her. Something told him that Dorian Gray could not be trusted.

'Just know one thing,' said James. 'If he ever does anything to hurt you, he will have *me* to answer to.'

Sibyl smiled at her brother and reached up to kiss his cheek. 'Don't worry about me, big brother. I've found my very own Prince Charming – that's what I like to call him. My life is going to be perfect.'

Chapter Seven

Lord Henry stood in the small entrance of a shabby-looking theatre. It was in a part of town he did not go to very often and he recognised no one in the crowd of theatre-goers. That was until Basil walked through the doors, looking similarly out of place. They were both dressed in their usual theatre clothes, but compared to everyone else, their smart suits and bow ties stood out like a pair of diamonds in a box of peanuts.

'Thank goodness you're here!' said Lord Henry. 'Surely Dorian has given us the wrong address. This can't be the theatre his fiancée performs in, can it?'

'I'm afraid so,' replied Basil. 'He did say it was rather run down. Although I've heard the actors are good.'

At that moment, Dorian came rushing out to greet them. 'I am so glad you're here. Come, I have reserved the best seats in the house for us,' he said, ushering his two friends into the theatre. Their seats were in the middle of the audience. Dorian placed himself between Basil and Lord Henry.

'Thank you both for coming,'

he said. 'Sibyl is such a wonderful actress. You are about to witness something truly amazing. But more than that, she has shown me that there is more to life than just parties and beautiful things. Once I am married, I will have all I need!'

Before his friends could reply, the theatre lights went down and *Romeo and Juliet* began.

***

Two and a half hours later, Basil, Lord Henry and a stunned Dorian emerged from the theatre to stand under the glow of a street lamp.

'Well, that was … an *interesting* performance,' said Basil, trying to be kind.

'It's certainly not like anything I have seen before,' said Lord Henry, less kindly.

'I … I do not understand,' said Dorian. 'She was so perfect in every other play I saw her in. Truly, she lit up the stage!'

'Perhaps she was not feeling well?' suggested Basil, although he did not believe it. Of all the plays he had seen in his life, this one was by far the worst, and Sibyl was the worst actress in it.

'Or perhaps our young friend has been under a spell?' said Lord Henry, chuckling. 'The lady is very pretty … maybe that was what lit up the stage.'

Dorian shook his head. 'No, she was magnificent, a true acting talent!' he said, his voice rising with upset. 'I must go and see her. Something must be wrong!'

CHAPTER EIGHT

Sibyl's dressing room was small and smelled of damp, but it was filled with red roses sent by her fiancé. The rest of the cast were quite jealous of her.

She squealed with delight when Dorian came to see her after her performance. She had been waiting all night, wishing the play would go faster so she could see him again.

'My love! You are here!' she

said, jumping up to give him a hug. 'What did you think of the play?'

Dorian slowly sat down on one of the tatty, patched up armchairs. 'I did not like it,' he said.

'Oh well, Shakespeare can be a bit boring, but I hope you liked *me*, at least,' Sibyl replied, cheerfully.

'No,' Dorian replied. 'No, I did not.

You were different, Sibyl. It was as though you did not care at all. Juliet is supposed to be full of love for Romeo, but you showed him none at all.'

Sibyl surprised Dorian by laughing. 'Don't you see?' she said. 'All the love I have now is for *you*. I can't pretend to love someone on stage because my heart is now yours! It doesn't matter anyway. Once we are married, I won't have to act anymore. I'll be your wife!'

Dorian stared at Sibyl as a cold feeling began to spread through him. It was as though someone had poured a bucket of ice over his head, freezing his mind, his body and his heart. Sibyl was no longer perfect to him. In fact, he now realised that it wasn't Sibyl he had fallen in love with at all – it was the characters she played on stage. He was in love with someone who didn't exist.

'No ...' Dorian said at last. His voice was no louder than a whisper. 'No, you will not be my wife. I cannot marry you.'

Sibyl's face turned pale with shock. 'What?' she said. 'You don't mean that! You *can't* mean that.'

‘I’m sorry, Sibyl,’ Dorian said, standing up. His mind was made up and he could not stay in Sibyl’s dressing room a moment longer. ‘I do mean it. The marriage is off. I will leave you now and we shall never meet again.’

CHAPTER NINE

Dorian expected to feel sorry for breaking off his engagement to Sibyl, but he did not. He knew that it was the right thing to do.

He sat at home the following day, when his footman entered to announce the arrival of Lord Henry.

'Henry!' Dorian said. 'I'm glad you're here, I have some news.'

'As have I,' said Lord Henry, looking more serious than he

usually did. 'I'm sorry to tell you that Sibyl has died.'

Dorian was stunned into silence.

'A friend of mine passed the news on this morning,' Lord Henry continued. 'Apparently, she received some bad news last night and her heart could not take the shock.'

Dorian turned to stare into the fire. 'It was me,' he said, quietly. 'I broke off our engagement after the play. It must have been that news that killed her.'

Dorian was confused by his feelings. Sibyl had died and it was his fault. He *should* have felt terrible. He should have been upset, crying, begging God for forgiveness – but he wasn't.

Lord Henry took Dorian's arm and sat him down on the sofa. 'My dear boy, you can't blame yourself. Even if she did die of a broken heart, isn't that the ultimate gift of love?'

Lord Henry's words made sense to Dorian. Thanks to him, Sibyl had known love and happiness – at least for a while. He should not feel guilty about that.

'Thank you, my friend,' Dorian said. 'Yes, you are right. Quite right! Thank you for coming to tell me. I assure you I am well.'

After Lord Henry had gone, Dorian walked peacefully through his home. He admired the beautiful items he had collected. He admired his reflection in the large mirrors that hung over his fireplaces. Then he caught sight of the portrait that Basil had painted of him. Something seemed different about it. As he looked closer, he saw that instead of the calm expression he had worn when he sat for the painting, his mouth in the portrait was now twisted into a sneer.

Chapter Ten

When Dorian woke up the next morning he went straight to his portrait. Had he been dreaming? Had the portrait really changed?

It had.

Dorian stared at his own face, sneering nastily back at him. He was so disturbed by the picture that he grabbed a lace tablecloth and threw it over the frame to hide it.

Later that morning, Basil Hallward was shown into Dorian's

drawing room. 'How are you, my boy?' said Basil. 'Henry told me the news about Sibyl and I just had to come and see you.'

'I appreciate the thought,' said Dorian. 'But truly, I'm fine.'

Basil looked confused. 'Fine? But your fiancée has died, Dorian, you can't be *fine*.'

Dorian let out a small laugh. 'Oh, I assure you, I can be,' he said. 'Sibyl and I were not meant for each other. If her heart could not take that fact, it is not my fault.'

Basil stared at Dorian, horrified. Although he looked the same, Basil sensed a change in the young man. Something about his personality had twisted. He seemed cruel and unfeeling. Perhaps spending so much time with Lord Henry had made him this way. But even Basil had to admit that he had never seen Lord Henry act as uncaring as this.

Basil cleared his throat and said, 'I see. Well, in that case there is something else I wanted to see you about. Your portrait. Would you allow me to display it in a gallery?'

Dorian's eyes widened for just a moment. 'My portrait?' he said, a little nervously. ‘I thought you said it was mine to keep.’

‘It is,’ replied Basil. ‘But nothing I have painted since has been half as good. It would mean a lot if I could show it to the public.’

‘No,’ Dorian replied. He could not let Basil see the painting because the painting had changed, and Dorian had a feeling he knew why. ‘No, you can’t have the painting. It’s mine and I don’t want it to be displayed.’

Basil was disappointed and confused by this rejection. He made his excuses to leave Dorian's house as soon as he could. With Basil gone, Dorian ripped the painting off the wall and carried it up to the dusty attic at the top of his large house.

For a moment he paused, regretting for just a second that he did not tell Basil the real reason why he would not let him display his portrait. Perhaps Basil could have helped him.

The thought did not last long. 'Basil saw me as a beautiful young man when he painted this,' said Dorian. 'And a beautiful young man I shall remain!'

Chapter Eleven

From that day on, Dorian began to see a change in himself – not his actual, flesh-and-blood self, but his painted self in the portrait. He realised that no matter what he did, what he ate, what he drank or how badly he behaved, he woke each morning looking exactly as he had when Basil painted him.

The portrait, however, *did* change. Over time the hair became patchy, the face developed warts and the features twisted.

After a year or so, Dorian grew tired of London. He saw less and less of his old friends. Basil was concerned about Dorian's behaviour, so Dorian stayed away from him. Lord Henry still admired Dorian's ability to look perfect no matter what, but Dorian was getting bored of him, too.

Dorian decided to travel. He had plenty of money and nothing to do with his time, so it made perfect sense. Now and then, he sent postcards to Lord Henry, with wild stories about where he was and what he was up to. He didn't bother to send anything to Basil, as he knew his old friend would only disapprove.

Basil heard the stories anyway, from Lord Henry at first, then from the gossips in London and even occasionally from reading them in the newspapers. He remembered the polite, friendly young man Dorian had once been. But, as the years passed, he realised that young man was gone.

***

It was almost eighteen years since Dorian had first sat in Basil's studio, ready to have his portrait painted. After a lovely, quiet afternoon at the National Gallery, Basil was returning home when he saw a figure on the pavement that he thought he recognised. But it couldn't be … Could it?

Dorian Gray stood by a large carriage with luggage around his feet. It was as though he had been frozen in time.

Despite being eighteen years older, he looked exactly the same.

Chapter Twelve

'Dorian Gray? Is that you?' Basil asked, in case the young man in front of him was a younger relative of Dorian's, which would make a lot more sense.

'Basil Hallward!' said Dorian, grasping Basil's hand to shake it warmly. 'Who would have thought that one of the first people I met back in London would be you.'

'It is Dorian, isn't it?' Basil asked again, still unable to believe it. Dorian had not changed at all. There was not a wrinkle on his face nor a grey hair on his head, whereas Basil, who was almost sixty, had both. Dorian would be nearly forty years old by now, and yet he looked no more than twenty.

'Of course, it's me!' Dorian laughed. 'Listen, I'm a little busy right now getting settled back in, but why don't you come around for dinner tonight?'

Basil nodded, unable to speak, as Dorian continued to get his luggage out of the carriage.

***

Basil had not been to Dorian's London house for nearly twenty years. In that time, it had grown full of items from his travels. They had travelled back ahead of Dorian, just as rumours of his bad behaviour had done. From wild parties, to stealing, to promising to marry a whole string of young women only to leave them as he had left Sibyl, the rumours were not favourable. And yet, somehow Dorian had got away with it all. He was never in the paper for being arrested, and it looked as though he still had plenty of money.

Basil was shown into Dorian's living room. It was filled with large artwork, expensive-looking antiques and grand furniture. It reminded Basil of Lord Henry's drawing room, although this was even more over the top.

'You've decorated,' said Basil, taking a seat in a large armchair as he sipped his drink from a crystal glass.

'I find that I must be surrounded by beautiful things, Basil,' said Dorian. 'Otherwise, what is the point of life?'

‘Have you enjoyed your travels?’ Basil asked.

‘More than I can begin to describe! I have done nothing for eighteen years but please myself.’

Basil frowned. ‘That sounds … lovely,’ he managed. ‘I am about to go to Paris for a few weeks to paint.’

‘Paris is simply wonderful!’ said Dorian. ‘There are so many beautiful women and the most delicious foods.’

‘But before I go, I feel I must tell you that there have been stories about you,’ said Basil.

'Terrible stories about your behaviour abroad. I must ask, is any of it true?'

Dorian smiled wickedly. 'All of it, I imagine.'

CHAPTER THIRTEEN

Basil stared as Dorian proudly admitted that the horrible rumours were true. 'But why, Dorian?' Basil asked. 'Why would you do such things?'

'Because I wanted to!' laughed Dorian. 'Because I *could*. I'm enjoying the world as I please like Henry said, and I don't feel bad about it. I'm happy. I know that no matter what I do, I will always be young and beautiful.'

'What makes you so sure?' Basil asked, a little angrily. 'How do you know that one day you won't be arrested or become ill because of your unhealthy lifestyle? How do you know that your hair won't go grey and your body won't tire?'

Dorian smiled. 'Do you really want to know how?' he asked. 'I suppose out of anyone in the world, you should be the one to see it.'

'To see what?' Basil asked.

'The portrait, of course!'

Dorian finished his drink in one gulp before placing it on a silver tray. 'The portrait is the key to everything. Follow me!'

Basil followed Dorian up staircase after staircase and into Dorian's dusty attic. Cobwebs filled the air as they made their way past boxes and crates, to where a familiar frame was mounted on a stand and covered by a lace cloth.

In the years since Dorian had left London, Basil had not painted anything as good as this portrait. He was offended to find that Dorian was not even displaying it.

'I don't understand,' said Basil. 'Do you no longer like the painting? Why is it hidden away up here?'

'Oh, I like the painting very much,' said Dorian with a smile. 'Tell me, do you like it as much as you once did?'

Dorian pulled the lace cloth off the painting to reveal a hideous, monstrous face underneath. The features, once handsome, were now disfigured and overgrown. The skin was full of warts. The hair was missing in parts and matted in others. The expression on the face was so terrible that Basil had to look away.

‘What have you done to it?’ asked Basil, when he was finally able to speak.

‘I have not touched it since the day you gave it to me,’ Dorian said. ‘Come, take a closer look, don’t be afraid.’

Basil approached the painting slowly, as though it might come alive if he moved too quickly. He forced himself to examine the paint and the brushstrokes. It was still his painting, he was sure of that, but how had it changed so dramatically?

Chapter Fourteen

Dorian looked pleased with himself as he threw the lace cloth over the painting once more. 'You see, Basil,' he began, 'it all started with Sibyl. After she died, I noticed the first change in the painting. A small difference in the mouth. It was the reason I did not want you to display it.'

Basil remembered the day clearly; Dorian had shown no remorse or sadness at Sibyl's passing.

'I noticed that whatever I did, however selfish or unkind I was, I felt no guilt,' Dorian said. 'I felt fine. The portrait, however, continued to change.'

'I don't understand,' said Basil, although he was starting to. Somehow, the painting had changed instead of Dorian. Just the thought of such dark magic made him tremble with fear.

'As the years went by, I stayed looking exactly as I did on the day you finished my portrait,' Dorian continued. 'Young and handsome.

Then I realised that it all started on that day – the day I wished that my portrait could grow old instead of me. Do you remember? Well … my wish came true!'

Basil shook his head violently. 'This is not right …' he said. 'No man can live a life doing exactly as he chooses, never caring about who he hurts.'

Dorian laughed, and it sent shivers down Basil's spine.

'As long as my portrait

exists, that is exactly what I will continue to do!'

Basil felt a surge of energy build up inside him. If he had created the portrait, then he should be the one to destroy it. Somehow, its power had warped the nice young man Dorian had once been. He was now as ugly on the inside as he was beautiful on the outside. If the portrait was destroyed, its power would surely disappear.

Basil frantically looked around the attic until he spotted a broken bottle. In a flash, he grabbed it and lunged for the painting, determined to shred it to pieces.

'No!' cried Dorian when he realised what Basil was trying to do. He grabbed Basil's arms and the two men struggled, knocking over boxes and fighting over control of the broken bottle's sharp, jagged edges.

Physically, Dorian was still young and strong.

It was easy for him to overpower his friend, who was much older. Basil lurched backwards; the bottle flew from his hand. Stumbling over a pile of old books, he fell. He didn't get up again.

Dorian watched, breathing heavily, as the painter gasped twice, then was silent.

'Basil?' he said. There was no answer. There was no movement – not even a rise and fall of his chest. The broken bottle was nowhere to be seen, as if Basil had fallen on top of it.

He was dead.

Chapter Fifteen

Afterwards, Dorian did not think much about the dreadful events in his attic, or the lifeless body of his friend. He simply straightened his clothes, smoothed his hair and went about his business. He told himself that nothing bad would come of Basil's death; the portrait would change, but he would go on as he had before.

News of Dorian's return to London had spread. A few days

later, he was invited to dinner at Agatha Henry's house, for which he dressed in his finest clothes and set out.

As soon as he entered Agatha Henry's dining room, he felt a wave of satisfaction wash over him. The other dinner guests looked shocked by his youthful, handsome appearance. Dorian smiled at their reaction and took his seat next to an ageing Lord Henry, who gazed at him open-mouthed.

'Dorian Gray?' he said in disbelief – and more than a little envy. 'The years have been far kinder to you than to me!'

Dorian laughed with false modesty. 'I have you to thank,' he said. 'I remember you said once that we would all be happier if we never felt bad about anything. I have lived by that rule for nearly twenty years, enjoying everything the world has to offer.'

Lord Henry was surprised that his advice had been so well remembered. 'It has done you no harm, I see,' he said. 'Despite old Basil's warning. You look wonderful!'

'I *feel* wonderful!' said Dorian. But as the words left his mouth,

he realised that they weren't true. A strange feeling bubbled in the pit of his stomach at the mention of the painter's name. He had been so used to living life without a care in the world that he did not recognise it straight away. Then, as the evening went on, and neither food nor drink settled his stomach, he realised what the feeling was. It was guilt.

'I'm afraid I must be leaving,' Dorian said, abruptly standing up and addressing the rest of the dinner guests.

'But, my dear fellow, you have not had your dessert yet,' said Lord Henry, placing a hand on Dorian's arm.

'I must go at once,' Dorian said, a bead of sweat appearing on his otherwise perfect face. 'I do apologise.' With that, Dorian left Agatha Henry's house.

He did not want to go home. The thought of the painting in his attic and the memory of what had happened there was crowding his brain. The guilt was something he had not experienced in many, many years. He walked the streets of London until he realised where he had ended up. It was the theatre where Sibyl used to perform. The little café that stood next door was still open, so Dorian slipped inside.

Chapter Sixteen

The café was busy and the air was hot and stuffy. Dorian found a small table next to the window and sat down. He smudged the glass with his sleeve to look out at the street and think about his life. He had everything any person could ever want. He had the ability to stay young forever. The ability to do whatever he wanted without any physical consequences. So why was he feeling this way?

Basil's face jumped to the front of Dorian's mind. Basil had been his friend once, and Dorian had watched him die without trying to help. He did not like the way that made him feel.

'Can I get you anything, sir?'

Dorian jumped as a waitress appeared at his table, ready to take his order.

'Oh, erm, just a cup of tea, please,' Dorian said. The waitress did not move. She stared at Dorian for a moment or two, taking in his face and clothes. Dorian was used to being stared at by strangers, but the look on the waitress's face was confusion.

'Lord, it's Prince Charming!' she said.

Dorian had not been called that name for many years. 'I'm sorry?' he said.

'Prince Charming! Sibyl's fiancé!' the waitress declared, so loudly that many of the other café-goers looked over at them. 'Poor Sibyl,' she said, shaking her head. Then, as though suddenly remembering, she added: 'Hang about, wasn't it *you* who broke her heart? Broke it so badly she died the very same night?'

Dorian put on his best smile. 'I'm sorry, madam, you are mistaken,' he lied. 'I have never been to this part of town before. Perhaps you wouldn't mind fetching my tea now?'

The waitress frowned and left the table. Before she reached the kitchen to place Dorian's order, however, she was stopped by a man in a tattered Royal Navy uniform.

'What did you just call that man?' he asked. 'The one over by the window.'

'Him?' the waitress said, looking back at Dorian. 'He looks just like a man my old friend Sibyl was engaged to. She called him Prince Charming – but he says he's not.'

The sailor did not wait to hear the rest of the waitress's story. He stormed over to the table and picked Dorian up by his collar.

'YOU!' he growled. 'You broke my Sibyl's heart! You *killed* her!'

Chapter Seventeen

Dorian knew at once who the man was. He had seen pictures of him in Sibyl's dressing room, pinned to her make-up mirror. It was James Vane, Sibyl's brother – although he was now much older, and his years at sea had made him rough.

'I … I don't know who Sibyl is!' Dorian lied, struggling to get free of James's grasp.

‘Sibyl is the girl you asked to marry you eighteen years ago,’ James said, pushing Dorian against the window. ‘My sister. The woman you abandoned. The woman you destroyed!’

Dorian’s mind raced. Just as he thought he was about to be pushed *through* the window, he said: ‘Sir, look at me. How old do you think I am?’

James loosened his grip on Dorian a little.

‘You say your sister died eighteen years ago,’ Dorian continued. ‘Well, I am only twenty years old. How could I possibly have known her?'

James let go and took a step back to study Dorian. He was a young man, he realised. He certainly did not look as though he was nearly forty. The waitress must have made a mistake.

Now free, Dorian took his chance to leave. James stood in silence, watching him through the misted glass of the café window.

'I don't care what he says,' said the waitress, appearing behind James. 'That was Prince

CAFE

Charming all right. That was Dorian Gray.'

***

Thoughts crowded Dorian's mind; thoughts he had not had for many, many years. To stop himself thinking of Basil and Sibyl, or the look on James Vane's face, he decided to organise a party in the countryside. He would get away from London. Away from the portrait.

The party was arranged for that very weekend. A selection

of London's most fashionable people arrived at the large country house that Dorian's grandfather had once owned. The guests settled into their rooms and then gathered in the drawing room.

'To a weekend full of fun!' declared Dorian, raising his glass. 'We shall eat and dance tonight. I have planned a hunt for tomorrow.'

The guests cheered and clinked their glasses together. Already, Dorian was starting to feel better.

A few moments later, Lord Henry's arrival was announced.

‘Henry!’ Dorian said, throwing an arm around his friend. ‘I’m glad you could make it.’

‘Thank you,’ replied Lord Henry. ‘Have you invited Basil, too? He will be so glad to hear you are back in England.’

Dorian’s smile fell. ‘No … he …’ Dorian began. ‘He is in Paris.’

‘That’s right!’ said Lord Henry. ‘Oh, I have to warn you, Dorian, I think you might have an uninvited guest trying to get in. I saw a man in shabby-looking clothes wandering about outside.’

‘Nonsense, we keep the gates

firmly closed – good lord!' Dorian cried, dropping his glass and staring, eyes wide, at the drawing-room window. 'I saw a face!'

Dorian's footmen went outside to investigate, but Dorian knew exactly who the face belonged to. It was James Vane. Somehow, Sibyl's brother had followed him.

Chapter Eighteen

That night, Dorian found it hard to sleep. When he did manage to close his eyes, his dreams were filled with faces from the past – each one telling him to mend his ways.

In the morning, he led the guests out into the fields, ready to hunt pheasants and rabbits.

Dorian did not feel like talking very much, so he wandered away from the group, and into a patch of woodland on the edge of his land. He found a tree stump and sat on it for a while, collecting his thoughts. Eventually, out of the corner of his eye, he spotted movement.

It was a tall, proud hare with ears like velvet and two dark brown eyes that looked straight into Dorian's.

'How beautiful,' Dorian sighed, not even thinking about picking up his gun. An animal as sweet and innocent as this did not deserve to come to any harm.

'It went this way!' said a voice in the near distance.

'Are you sure?' said another.

Just then, two members of Dorian's party came trudging into the woodland. 'Hello Dorian, have you spotted a hare? We thought we saw one just now.'

Dorian stood up and glanced in the direction of the hare. He was suddenly terrified that his friends would shoot the poor creature.

'NO,' said Dorian, forcefully.

'You mean you haven't seen the hare?'

'I mean you can't shoot it!' said Dorian.

The men laughed. 'That's not like you, Dorian!' said one. 'Why do you suddenly care whether or not the creature lives?'

'Look! Look! There it is!' said the other, swinging his gun round to take a shot. As the bullet fired, Dorian was gripped with terror. He did not want anything else to die because of him. His heart, which had stopped feeling anything for anyone long ago, suddenly burst with worry and fear.

'You missed!' said one of the men, pointing at the hare. It bounded away as fast as it could. Dorian breathed a sigh of relief, his hands shaking at his sides.

'ARGH!' a scream sounded from within the woods. A few moments later, one of Dorian's footmen came running from the trees towards him.

'Mr Gray, sir, come quickly,' said the footman. 'Someone has been shot.'

Chapter Nineteen

Dorian sat with his head in his hands. Tears flowed down his perfectly smooth face. He was back in his London drawing room, sitting alone by the fire.

He had cut his country house party short after the death in the woods. A man had been shot by a bullet meant for the beautiful hare. When they brought the body back to the house, Dorian had been horrified to see that it was James Vane.

'Dead,' Dorian had whispered, staring at James. 'Because of me. Another person dead. Because. Of. Me.'

Days had passed since Dorian returned to London, but he had not left his house. He could not eat, or sleep, and he refused to see anyone or go anywhere. Scenes from the last eighteen years of his life danced around his head. He saw the people he had been rude to. The parties he had gone to without being invited. The antiques he had stolen when he was told they were not for sale.

He saw Sibyl, so young and innocent, so full of love for him – and what had he given her in return? He had treated her like an object to be forgotten about when it no longer interested him.

He saw Basil. His friend who had painted his portrait. He had not deserved to die in pain.

He saw James. All he had wanted was for his beloved sister to be happy and safe, and Dorian had taken that away from him. Now he was dead too.

Dorian paced his living room, running his hands through his hair until it was unusually messy. He knocked candelabras off their stands, pulled art off the walls. None of these beautiful things mattered anymore. Nothing could make him feel better.

He caught sight of himself in the huge mirror above his fireplace. Even after days of crying and no sleep, his face looked perfect. It made Dorian feel sick. Then it struck him. The portrait. Everything that had happened to him in the last eighteen years was all down to the portrait!

Dorian tore up the stairs and into his attic. He pulled the lace cloth off the frame and gasped. The portrait had become more hideous than he could ever have imagined. The eyes were black, sunken holes and the hands were covered in blood.

Dorian grabbed the broken bottle that had killed Basil and began to tear into the painting. Dorian shredded every inch of the canvas, until nothing remained.

***

Days later, Lord Henry stood at the door to Dorian's attic, waiting for the footman to open it.

'I don't know what to tell you, sir,' said the footman. 'The last we saw of Mr Gray he was in his drawing room. He had not left the house for days.'

'Well, since he went missing, we have searched everywhere for him,' said Lord Henry. 'He's not in the country and no one has seen him. This is the only place we haven't looked.'

The footman opened the door and Lord Henry stepped inside. 'There!' he said, noticing a figure on the ground. The figure was wearing Dorian's clothes, but as Lord Henry rolled him over, he saw the face of a deformed, sickly old man. A man with striking blue eyes. A man who looked closer to ninety than forty – much less twenty.

'It's Dorian,' gasped Lord Henry. 'It's Dorian Gray!'

AUTHOR BIOGRAPHY

OSCAR WILDE

Oscar Wilde was born in Dublin in 1854. He later moved to London where he published a range of poems, plays and fairy tales. *The Picture of Dorian Gray* was his only novel. Wilde's personal life was colourful but tragic. He was gay in a time when it was illegal, and he went to prison for it. Today he is one of the most quoted writers, including 'Be yourself; everyone else is already taken'.